HEARTSTRINGS

LIVIA XIA WANG

Copyright © Livia Xia Wang
All Rights Reserved.

This book has been self-published with all reasonable efforts taken to make the material error-free by the author. No part of this book shall be used, reproduced in any manner whatsoever without written permission from the author, except in the case of brief quotations embodied in critical articles and reviews.

The Author of this book is solely responsible and liable for its content including but not limited to the views, representations, descriptions, statements, information, opinions and references ["Content"]. The Content of this book shall not constitute or be construed or deemed to reflect the opinion or expression of the Publisher or Editor. Neither the Publisher nor Editor endorse or approve the Content of this book or guarantee the reliability, accuracy or completeness of the Content published herein and do not make any representations or warranties of any kind, express or implied, including but not limited to the implied warranties of merchantability, fitness for a particular purpose. The Publisher and Editor shall not be liable whatsoever for any errors, omissions, whether such errors or omissions result from negligence, accident, or any other cause or claims for loss or damages of any kind, including without limitation, indirect or consequential loss or damage arising out of use, inability to use, or about the reliability, accuracy or sufficiency of the information contained in this book.

Made with ♥ on the Notion Press Platform
www.notionpress.com

Contents

Contents

Preface

"Heartstrings" is a poignant narrative weaving the lives of Yuvan and Karan, whose love resonates like a timeless melody. From a chance encounter to a deep bond, their journey is a symphony of emotions, trials, and enduring commitment. As they face life's challenges together, their love proves unyielding, a testament to the profound connection they share. "Heartstrings" is a testament to the resilience of love, highlighting the transformative power of a relationship that touches the deepest chords of the heart.

Acknowledgements

I would like to express my heartfelt gratitude to all those who have been a part of this journey with me. To my family, for their unwavering support and encouragement, and for always believing in me. To my friends, for their endless love and inspiration. To my readers, for embracing my stories and allowing them to touch your hearts. And to the universe, for guiding me and blessing me with the opportunity to share my words with the world. Thank you, from the bottom of my heart.

CHAPTER I

An Enchanting Reunion

Yuvan arrived at the lobby of the office complex with his twin boys Ishan and Jay. They were a delightful sight, engrossed in their playful chatter and interactions with their father. The children quickly caught the attention of the people in the lobby.

Approaching the reception, Yuvan requested, "Hi, good afternoon. Could you please connect me to the GM?"

The newly appointed receptionist replied, "Good afternoon, sir. I'm sorry, but visiting hours are over. Have you taken any appointments?"

Just then, a familiar voice called out from the back, "Hello, twins! How are you?" It was the secretary, Miss Hazel.

Jay responded, "We are good, thank you. We came to pick up Daddy. Can we go in?"

"Of course, you can. Come on, what are you waiting for?" the secretary replied with a smile.

Yuvan declined, saying, "It's okay, Miss Hazel. He is coming down to the lobby. Thanks anyway."

As they waited, Yuvan engaged in a brief conversation with Miss Hazel.

She asked, "How are you, Yuvan? How long is your vacation?"

Yuvan replied, "I'm doing well, thank you. I will be here for the entire month."

The twins' joyful voices filled the lobby as they called out to their dad. Karan smiled warmly and knelt down to hug Ishan and Jay, their excitement palpable. Yuvan, tall and handsome, approached from behind, his presence commanding yet gentle. He joined the group, and together, they made their way home, their bond evident in the way they interacted, with laughter and affection.

As they left, the receptionist couldn't help but notice the strong connection between Yuvan, Karan, and the twins. She turned to Miss Hazel, intrigued by the family dynamics she had just witnessed. Miss Hazel, who had known them for years, smiled knowingly, understanding the receptionist's curiosity.

"They have such a beautiful family," the receptionist remarked, still watching them leave.

"Yes, they do," Miss Hazel replied, her eyes following the family as they disappeared from view. "They are truly special."

Later, Miss Hazel explained to the receptionist, "He knew you are new. He just came to check on your performance."

The receptionist, curious, asked, "I think I messed up with him. Can I ask who that handsome guy with the children?"

"He is the GM's husband," Miss Hazel said, her voice carrying a hint of intrigue, knowing she was about to share something extraordinary.

The receptionist's eyes widened in surprise. "Eeh?" she exclaimed, momentarily taken aback by this revelation.

"Yes, you heard it right. They've been married for six years," Miss Hazel confirmed, a soft smile playing on her lips as she watched the receptionist process this information.

The receptionist's astonishment grew. "Wow, that's amazing," she murmured, her curiosity piqued.

"And the twins were born through a surrogate mother," Miss Hazel added, her eyes reflecting a deep admiration for the family she was describing.

The receptionist's eyes widened even further, captivated by the story unfolding before her. "I'm very interested in hearing more about them. This is the first time I've encountered a family like this," she admitted, her voice filled with genuine curiosity.

Miss Hazel, recognizing the receptionist's fascination, smiled warmly. "They're quite a remarkable family, indeed. Let me tell you their story..." She began, painting a vivid picture of Yuvan, Karan, and their beautiful family, weaving together a tale of love, commitment, and the joy of parenthood.

CHAPTER II

An Unexpected Encounter

The campus buzzed with excitement as Yuvan Reddy, a charismatic and multi-talented student, took the stage with his bandmates Aditya, Neel, and Raj. Yuvan, known for his musical prowess and adventurous spirit, stood out not only for his talents but also for his charming demeanor. Tall and striking, with sleek black hair and dimpled cheeks, he effortlessly captured the attention of everyone around him.

Beyond his musical abilities, Yuvan was also skilled in martial arts and had a unique talent for identifying ingredients by taste alone, a skill he inherited from his mother, Anjili Reddy. His father, Sanjay Reddy, added a touch of mystery to his background, being an investigation officer in the CBI.

As the performance ended, Yuvan retreated backstage with his friends. It was then that he was approached by a new face—Karan Gupta, a freshman in Business Management. Karan, though reserved and troubled, was drawn to Yuvan's performance and mustered the courage to introduce himself.

"Hi, I'm Karan. Your performance was incredible. I enjoyed every moment of it," Karan said warmly, extending his hand in admiration.

"Thank you," Yuvan replied with a genuine smile, shaking Karan's hand.

"If you don't mind, can I ask you something?" Karan inquired politely.

"Of course," Yuvan replied, curious about what Karan wanted to know.

With a smile, Karan asked, "How did you get the scar on your forehead?"

Yuvan chuckled, recalling the mishap. "Ah, that was from a boomerang incident during practice. Why do you ask?"

"I wanted to confirm that you're the person I've been searching for these past 12 years," Karan revealed, surprising Yuvan.

"What do you mean? Who are you exactly?" Yuvan asked, intrigued.

But before Karan could explain, Esther Thompson, Yuvan's childhood friend and college beauty, interrupted.

"Looks like you're busy. We can talk later," Karan said, handing Yuvan a lollipop before leaving.

"Wait, I didn't finish," Yuvan exclaimed, but Karan, with a smile on his face, left, leaving Yuvan puzzled.

Turning to his friends, Yuvan expressed his confusion. "Who is he? Do you know him?"

"No, I don't," Yuvan replied, his voice tinged with curiosity and intrigue. "But there was something about him...something familiar yet unknown."

"Why do you care if you don't know him?" Esther asked, her tone gentle as she picked up the lollipop from Yuvan.

"The way he talked to me, it bothers me," Yuvan explained to Esther and his friends.

"Well, let's find out more about him. Don't dwell on it," one of his friends consoled Yuvan.

Meanwhile, Esther discreetly disposed of the lollipop in the trash without anyone noticing.

CHAPTER III

Unforeseen Connection

One day, Karan found himself driving back to his dorm in his XUV after a visit to his parents. While waiting at a signal, a sleek superbike pulled up next to him, catching his eye. The biker, with a swift motion, lifted the helmet shutter, revealing himself to be Yuvan.

Captivated by the impressive bike, Karan couldn't help but admire it.

Karan rolled down his window and greeted Yuvan with a friendly, "Hi, good morning."

"Good morning. Where have you been?" Yuvan asked, curious.

"I went to visit my parents. I'm heading back to the dorm," Karan replied.

"Okay," Yuvan nodded.

"Where are you staying?" Karan inquired politely.

"I'm staying in a condo, a few kilometers away," Yuvan replied.

"Alone?" Karan asked casually.

"Yes, why?" Yuvan inquired, curious about the question.

"No, just curious," Karan clarified, smiling.

Their conversation flowed smoothly, each question and response revealing a bit more about each other, creating a brief but meaningful connection.

"Why do you have a boomerang on the dashboard?" Yuvan asked curiously, noting the unusual choice of decoration.

"Oh, that's my confidence booster, my everything," Karan replied with a smile, indicating the significance of the boomerang to him.

"Do you know how to use it?" Yuvan inquired, fascinated by Karan's attachment to the boomerang.

"No, but someone I know does," Karan replied casually, leaving Yuvan spellbound yet again.

Before Yuvan could delve deeper into the conversation, the signal turned green, signaling their need to part ways. Yuvan headed towards his condo while Karan continued on to his dorm. Their brief exchange at the signal felt like a pleasant interruption in the monotony of the day.

During his ride to the condo, Yuvan found his thoughts consumed by Karan and the mysterious boomerang. "That boomerang looks familiar, like the one I lost in my childhood. The color is the same too. Do I actually know him? Who was he talking about, the person who knows how to use a boomerang? Who is he, actually? He is getting on my nerves."

As Yuvan contemplated these thoughts, he realized he missed an opportunity to learn more about Karan. "I would have asked for his number. Never mind, I might see him at college," he reassured himself as he arrived at his condo, his mind still filled with questions about the intriguing encounter.

Later, at college, Yuvan approached his friends and inquired, "Do any of you have any information about Karan?"

"No, but we will look into it soon," one of his friends replied, showing willingness to help.

Esther, however, in a slightly disappointed tone, asked, "Why do you want to bother?"

Yuvan explained, "I just want to know. He's getting on my nerves."

His friends nodded understandingly, indicating their readiness to assist in finding out more about Karan.

"By the way, did you bring the notes?" Yuvan asked Esther, changing the subject.

"Of course, yes. Here," Esther handed the notes to Yuvan.

CHAPTER IV

"The Intriguing News"

One evening, as they sat on the campus grounds, engrossed in conversation, one of Yuvan's friends, Neel, suddenly dashed towards them, his face beaming with excitement. "Neel, relax, what's the matter?" Yuvan asked, curious by his friend's enthusiasm.

"I've got some information about Karan," Neel exclaimed, barely able to contain his excitement.

"What? Tell me everything," Yuvan urged, eager to learn more about the enigmatic Karan. "He is the only son of the business tycoon, Arvind Gupta. Born with a silver spoon, he doesn't have many friends. His only close friend is Tej Mehta, who is also a faculty member in the Business department," Neel revealed, his words sparking a mix of awe and curiosity among the group.

"Wow, that's quite something," they all exclaimed in unison, impressed by Karan's background.

"But how does he know me? What's the connection?" Yuvan pondered aloud, the mystery deepening.

They all exchanged puzzled glances, unable to provide an answer.

"Well, if anyone might know more, it would be Tej. He might have some insights," Raj suggested, breaking the silence.

"I have a friend who stays in the dorm. We can ask him if he knows anything," Aditya offered, eager to help unravel the mystery.

"Then let's proceed," Yuvan agreed, determined to uncover the truth behind Karan's connection to him.

CHAPTER V

The Beginning: Numbers and Sketches

Two days later, after class, Yuvan and his friends were engrossed in conversation when Aditya suddenly interrupted.

"My friend in the dorm couldn't find any information, but he managed to get Karan's phone number," Aditya announced, a mischievous glint in his eyes.

"Wow, that's fantastic! Give it to me," Yuvan exclaimed, his excitement palpable. Aditya chuckled.

"No, you should treat us if you want the number," he teased.

"Of course, yes, count on me," Yuvan replied eagerly, willing to do whatever it took to get Karan's contact information. "Pick a restaurant, share the location. The treat is on me. See you for dinner. I have work today," Yuvan said as he departed, his mind buzzing with anticipation.

Later, after finishing his work, Yuvan headed to the restaurant where his friends had gathered. They enjoyed a delightful dinner, filled with laughter and good food, as Yuvan eagerly awaited the opportunity to contact Karan. After reaching home, Yuvan messaged Karan, initiating their first direct conversation.

"Hi, it's me Yuvan," he wrote, breaking the ice.

"How did you get my number?" Karan asked, clearly intrigued by the unexpected message.

"Just like that," Yuvan replied casually, not revealing the dinner deal with his friends.

"Are you spying on me?" Karan asked, a hint of humor in his question. Yuvan replied with a smiley emoji, indicating that he meant no harm.

"Did you have dinner?" Yuvan asked, trying to keep the conversation light and friendly.

"Of course, yes," Karan replied.

"Am I disturbing you?" Yuvan asked, mindful of not intruding on Karan's time.

"No, not at all. Did you have dinner?" Karan inquired.

"Yes, I went out with my friends for dinner," Yuvan shared, adding to the casual banter.

Karan then sent a picture he had drawn, surprising Yuvan. It was a detailed sketch of Yuvan on his bike at the signal.

"Wow, this is awesome! Nobody has ever drawn me like this," Yuvan expressed his admiration.

"Thank you so much. You are a talented artist. I loved it. You captured even the minute details. It's incredible. Can I have that drawing?" Yuvan requested, impressed by Karan's skill.

"No, it's for me. I will draw another and hand it over to you," Karan replied, showing his attachment to his creation.

"Why do you want to keep this drawing? Please sell it to me," Yuvan pleaded, eager to own the artwork.

"Well, this is not for sale. I will give you another picture of yours tomorrow. Where should I come to hand over my work?" Karan offered, suggesting a plan for the exchange.

"Tell me your class, I will come and collect it," Yuvan replied, agreeing to the arrangement.

"Okay, then good night. See you tomorrow," Yuvan bid farewell.

"Good night," Karan replied, ending their first conversation on a pleasant note.

CHAPTER VI

An Evening Invitation

The next morning, Karan woke up to a good morning message from Yuvan.

"Good morning, Yuvan. What's up?" Karan replied promptly.

"Did you finish the drawing?" Yuvan asked eagerly. "Hmm...why?" Karan responded, curious.

"Then dine with me tonight. I will share the location later. Is that okay with you?" Yuvan proposed.

"Yes, of course, deal," Karan agreed, feeling excited. "Well then, see you in the evening," Yuvan said cheerfully.

"Hmm..." Karan replied, already looking forward to the evening.

While Karan was texting, Tej, his friend, asked, "What is it? Whom are you texting?" "I told you yesterday, Yuvan asked for a drawing," Karan explained.

"Hmm..." Tej expressed, nodding in understanding.

"Well, he asked to hand it over at night. He is going to treat me. He will share the location later," Karan elaborated

. "Are you sure about it? Do I need to accompany you?" Tej inquired, concerned.

"It's okay, because it's Yuvan. I will call for help if I feel discomfort," Karan reassured him.

"Okay, cool," Tej said, trusting Karan's judgment.

After getting ready, both Karan and Tej went to class. Meanwhile, Yuvan's friends asked him whether he had called Karan yet.

"No, I just texted him. He shared a fantastic drawing with me, me riding the bike," Yuvan said proudly, showing the drawing to his friends.

"Actually, it is mind-blowing!" one of Yuvan's friends exclaimed, and they all praised Karan. Esther, one of Yuvan's friends, felt a pang of jealousy but didn't reveal it.

"I am going to invite him to a treat today," Yuvan announced.

"Well, that's great!" Aditya replied, and the other friends supported Yuvan's idea, except for Esther.

As the day unfolded, it was a beautiful day at the college. After class, Yuvan headed to work. Before starting his job, he texted Karan the location and the time. Yuvan's work finished at nine o'clock at night on weekdays. Karan agreed to meet him at nine o'clock, and Yuvan eagerly awaited their meeting.

›

CHAPTER VII

Unpredicted Interruptions

Karan arrived at the restaurant promptly at nine o'clock, leaving a note for Tej, who was showering, to inform him of his whereabouts and assure him that he would be back soon. He quickly checked his appearance in the mirror, running his fingers through his hair to ensure it was neat, before heading inside to meet Yuvan.

As he entered, the cozy ambiance welcomed him, and Yuvan's warm greeting added to the inviting atmosphere. "Welcome, Karan," Yuvan greeted with a smile that lit up the room.

"Thank you," Karan replied, feeling a sense of anticipation.

Yuvan led him to a table reserved just for them, overlooking a stunning view. "Come, take this seat. I reserved it for us," Yuvan said, pulling out a chair for Karan.

"Oh, that's thoughtful of you," Karan said, touched by the gesture, and took his seat. "Make yourself comfortable. Yours is the last order I'm taking today. Go through the menu and order when you are ready. I will wait," Yuvan said, gesturing towards the menu.

"Thank you," Karan replied, browsing the menu with interest. After a few moments, they placed their orders, and Yuvan joined Karan at the table.

"You're working here?" Karan asked, noticing Yuvan's ease in the restaurant.

"Yes, I do. It helps me fund my passion for adventure trips and exploring new places," Yuvan explained with a hint of excitement. "Would you like to join me sometime?"

"Thank you, but I'm not much of an adventure seeker," Karan replied with a chuckle.

"Why's that?" Yuvan inquired, genuinely curious.

"I'll tell you later. I don't want to spoil our evening," Karan said with a smile, wanting to keep the focus on their dinner.

Karan handed over the drawing to Yuvan, who was genuinely surprised and impressed by its quality. The drawing depicted the memorable concert Yuvan had played on the fresher's day.

"Wow, this is incredible! You're really talented," Yuvan praised, deeply touched by the thoughtful gift.

"Thank you," Karan replied, feeling a sense of pride in his work.

As they were about to start their meal, Esther arrived with another friend, surprising both Yuvan and Karan. Without asking, Esther joined their table, making Karan uncomfortable. He discreetly texted Tej for help. Karan's phone rang, and it was Tej.

"Excuse me, I want to take this call," Karan said, stepping outside the restaurant.

"I'm sorry, I have to go. Something came up. Thank you for the food. I'm so sorry that I can't join. Bye," Karan apologized as he returned to the table.

Yuvan, though disappointed, understood the situation. "Esther, why did you come now?" he asked, trying to hide his disappointment.

"We were just passing by. I didn't mean to intrude. I'm sorry," Esther explained, feeling apologetic.

"Just eat what you want and go home. I'm heading back home," Yuvan said, disappointed.

"Wait, I'm so sorry," Esther apologized again.

"It's okay," Yuvan said, leaving the restaurant.

As he left the restaurant, Yuvan couldn't help but feel a bit saddened by the unexpected turn of events. He took out his phone and texted Karan, apologizing for any discomfort caused and hoping for another opportunity to meet.

CHAPTER VIII

Beneath the Surface

The next day, as Yuvan and his friends chatted after lunch, a new face approached.

Excuse me, Yuvan. Hi, I'm Tej, Karan's friend. Can we talk?" Tej asked politely.

"Of course," Yuvan replied, leading Tej to a quieter spot.

"Yuvan, did anything happen yesterday while Karan was with you? He was fine when he left, but when he came back, he seemed disturbed. That's why I'm asking," Tej explained.

"Well, we were fine until Esther and her friend interrupted us. He got a call and had to leave in a hurry," Yuvan explained.

"I see. I've asked him several times, but he didn't reply. Now I am relieved. Thank you for your time. See you then," Tej said, preparing to leave.

"Wait, is he alright? Is there something I should know?" Yuvan inquired.

"Well, He's not your typical kid, as you might think. There are things that can disturb him quickly. So, when you invite him next time, make sure he's not in a crowded place. If he is, ensure he's comfortable. He's afraid of heights and not comfortable around females except his mom. He's still under medication and can have panic attacks," Tej explained.

"I'm sorry, I didn't know," Yuvan replied sadly.

"It's okay. You weren't aware," Tej reassured him.

"Can I ask you something else?" Yuvan asked.

"What do you want to know?" Tej replied.

"Has something happened to him before?" Yuvan asked.

"Yes, he was kidnapped when he was just five years old. It was a traumatic experience for him," Tej explained. Yuvan was stunned to hear about Karan's past.

"I'm so sorry to hear that. I never imagined," Yuvan said, shaken. "Just keep these things in mind. I shared because..." Tej paused.

"Because?" Yuvan prompted.

"He's been trying hard to overcome his struggles. And then he found you, his confidant," Tej explained.

"What are you talking about? This is all so confusing," Yuvan said, feeling lost. "The day he said he found me is still running in my head. I don't even remember if I know him."

"I can't tell you everything myself. I've shared enough. I found him comfortable with you in these twelve years, more than with anyone else," Tej said. "I know you have many questions. But I'm not the one to answer them. I'm sorry. See you around," Tej said, preparing to leave.

"Thank you for sharing this with me. I promise to keep it in mind," Yuvan replied.

"Yeah, I trust you and thank you for taking care of my friend yesterday," Tej expressed his gratitude.

Yuvan stood there, watching Tej walk away, his mind filled with confusion and questions.

CHAPTER IX

Echoes of Valor

Yuvan found himself in a challenging dilemma. Despite having assignments to submit and a mountain of studies awaiting him, his thoughts were completely consumed by Karan. No matter what he tried to focus on, Karan's plight overshadowed everything else, rendering him unable to concentrate. Even as he attempted to drift off to sleep, his mind was abuzz with unanswered questions.

"How does he know me? What is my connection to Karan? He mentioned searching for me for twelve years. If I was seven years old then, what was I doing?" These questions plagued Yuvan's thoughts, refusing to let him rest. Eventually, the weight of these inquiries lulled him into a restless sleep.

In Yuvan's dream, memories flooded back from twelve years ago. He was at the crowded amusement park with his mother, his boomerang tucked safely in his bag. The air was festive, filled with laughter and chatter. It was a lively evening at the amusement park, filled with the sounds of laughter and excitement.

Karan, a young boy holding hands with his mother, was joyfully exploring the various rides and attractions. Nearby, Yuvan and his mother were also enjoying the park's offerings. In a sudden turn of events, Karan found himself separated from his mother, surrounded by unfamiliar faces. Before anyone could react, he was whisked away in a van by unknown individuals.

Yuvan, witnessing the abduction, immediately sprang into action. He urged his mother to call the police and swiftly approached the van, employing his boomerang technique to create a distraction. With remarkable agility, Yuvan managed to slip into the van unnoticed. Inside, Yuvan instructed Karan to stay quiet and hid him beneath the last seat.

The kidnappers, puzzled by the sudden disturbance, hastily departed. Yuvan's father, a police officer, arrived at the scene, responding to the call from Yuvan's mother. Meanwhile, Karan's mother, distressed and frantic, searched desperately for her missing son. Yuvan's mother, filled with confidence in her son's abilities, offered comfort and support to Karan's mother during this trying time.

The kidnappers took Karan to an abandoned building, where they threatened to harm him if a ransom was not paid. While one of the kidnappers left to buy food, the other, a woman, cruelly beat Karan and drank excessively. Seizing an opportune moment, Yuvan emerged from his hiding spot and used his return boomerang to disarm the woman. With her incapacitated, Yuvan swiftly untied Karan and led him to safety.

As a token of remembrance, Yuvan gave his boomerang to Karan, who, in return, offered a lollipop from his pocket. Yuvan's heroic actions ensured Karan's safe return, a moment he later recollected in a dream.

In the quiet of the night, Yuvan woke from his dream, his heart still racing from the vivid memories. The clock read half past four, signaling the end of a stormy night. Despite the late hour, Yuvan found himself unable to sleep, his thoughts consumed by the events of that fateful day and the hope of one day reuniting with Karan.

It became evident to Yuvan why Karan harbored fears of crowds, heights, and discomfort around women. The traumatic kidnapping incident had etched deep scars in

Karan's young mind, leaving him with lasting emotional wounds.

The crowded amusement park, where he was separated from his mother and abducted, instilled in him a fear of crowds, a reminder of the chaos and helplessness he felt that day.

The threat of being thrown from the building's edge by the kidnappers fueled his fear of heights, a constant reminder of the danger he faced.

The brutal treatment by the woman kidnapper, who beat him and drank excessively, left him traumatized and wary of women, except for his mother.

Yuvan understood that these fears were not unfounded but rooted in a harrowing experience that had forever changed Karan's life.

CHAPTER X

Remembering You

The morning sun filtered through the curtains, casting a warm glow in the dorm room. Karan's phone buzzed, breaking the silence. He picked it up to see a message from Yuvan, saying he was waiting downstairs in the lobby.

Excitement surged through Karan as he jumped out of bed, quickly freshened up, and rushed down to the lobby. As he reached the bottom of the stairs, he saw Yuvan standing there. Karan froze, unable to move, his heart pounding in his chest. Yuvan noticed Karan and walked over to him.

Without a word, he pulled Karan into a tight hug. "I know very clearly now," Yuvan said softly, "why you are afraid of heights, why you don't want to be in crowded places, and why you are uncomfortable around women. I know now how you are connected to me. I know whose boomerang you have with you. I know why you gave me a lollipop on the freshman's day. You don't have to say a word. I'm so sorry I couldn't recognize you. I'm truly sorry."

Karan stood there, stunned, tears streaming down his cheeks.

Yuvan gently wiped Karan's tears away and said, "From now on, I will be with you always. You can count on me."

"Why did you take so long to remember me, huh?" Karan asked, his voice choked with emotion.

"I'm so sorry I forgot," Yuvan replied, sadness in his eyes. "Yesterday, it all came back to me while I was sleeping. I'm the only witness who saw how much you suffered,

Karan. I shouldn't have forgotten that. I'm so sorry."

"Enough, stop apologizing," Karan said, tears still flowing. He hugged Yuvan back, feeling a rush of emotions. Yuvan held him close, gently patting his soft, straight hair, comforting him in his moment of vulnerability.

From that day on, Yuvan and Karan's bond grew stronger. Yuvan was there for Karan, helping him overcome his fears and trauma. And Karan found solace in Yuvan's presence, knowing that he had someone who understood him completely. Their friendship blossomed, built on a foundation of trust, understanding, and a shared past that had finally come full circle. As they said their goodbyes, Karan knew that his life would never be the same again. He had found his long-lost friend, his missing piece, and he would never let him go.

CHAPTER XI

A Thoughtful Exchange

Amidst the hustle and bustle of a lively evening, Karan's phone buzzed persistently, creating a sense of urgency.In a moment of forgetfulness, Karan left his phone behind. Tej, with a hint of reluctance, answered the call in his place.

"Hello, This is Tej. Karan forgot to take his phone," Tej answered.

"Oh hi Tej, I'm sorry to bother you. He is not answering my calls or messages. I was worried," Yuvan explained.

"It's okay. He usually doesn't answer calls while practicing chess. Today, I'm not sure if he forgot his phone or intentionally left it," Tej replied thoughtfully.

"When do you think he'll be back?" Yuvan asked, his worry palpable.

"Probably around seven. I'll ask him to call you back," Tej assured him.

"No, it's alright. I'll call him back after work. I might not be able to answer any calls while on duty. Thank you, buddy," Yuvan said, grateful for the update.

"Is there a message you'd like me to pass on when he returns?" Tej offered kindly.

"No, it's fine. I just wanted to check if he could come to the restaurant where I work. Last time, things got mixed up. You remember that," Yuvan recalled.

"Yes, I remember. Just make sure Esther isn't there. He once mentioned she brings him bad luck. He really doesn't like her. Please don't mention this to him. I'm telling you this in confidence. I know she's your best friend," Tej confided.

"I understand. You can trust me. Thank you anyway. So, he's into chess," Yuvan noted, shifting the topic lightly.

"Yes, he's quite good at it. But he's never shown interest in competitions. I think he feels uncomfortable. I've never asked him about it," Tej shared.

"I appreciate your insights. I'll have to ask him about chess someday. Thank you for your help. See you soon, and take care," Yuvan concluded warmly, grateful for Tej's assistance and understanding.

CHAPTER XII

A Promise of Adventure

It was a pleasant surprise when Karan appeared at Yuvan's restaurant, the clock ticking half-past eight. A dark blue cap shielded part of Karan's face as he settled into a quiet corner, almost invisible to the rest of the world. Yuvan's eyes widened in disbelief and joy.

"Karan! Is that really you?" he exclaimed, his voice filled with emotion.

Karan looked up, a soft smile playing on his lips. "Yes, Yuvan, it's me," he replied, his eyes shimmering with unspoken stories.

"I can hardly believe it myself." "I noticed a flurry of missed calls and messages from you. Tej mentioned he answered the call on my behalf," Karan explained.

Yuvan, still in disbelief, managed a smile. "I'm glad you're here. What would you like to order?" he asked, eager to extend a warm welcome.

"Any fresh juice will do," Karan replied, his voice tinged with gratitude.

Within minutes, a glass of grape juice arrived at Karan's table, courtesy of Yuvan.

"Here's a treat from me. I'll be done with work by nine and then we can catch up properly," Yuvan offered.

"Thank you, Yuvan. I'll wait for you," Karan said, a sense of warmth in his tone.

As Yuvan finished his duties, he joined Karan at the table. Their conversation flowed effortlessly, filling the air with laughter and nostalgia.

Karan, curious, asked, "What prompted all the calls?"

"I wanted to make it up to you for the last time we met, and there was something else I wanted to ask," Yuvan replied, his gaze thoughtful.

"And what might that be?" Karan inquired, his eyes full of intrigue.

"I was hoping you'd join me on a one-day trip tomorrow, just the two of us. A small adventure," Yuvan proposed, his tone hopeful. Karan hesitated for a moment.

"I'm usually not one for adventures, and I have a doctor's appointment tomorrow evening. But I've already told my parents about finding you. They're eager to meet you. Will you come?" Karan asked, a mix of excitement and uncertainty in his voice.

After thinking it over, Yuvan eagerly agreed to Karan's offer of a one-day trip together. Karan, though a bit hesitant, ultimately agreed, intrigued by the idea.

They said their goodbyes, both looking forward to the adventure ahead, and went their separate ways, hearts hopeful for the new beginning their reunion promised.

CHAPTER XIII

A Homecoming Tale

Early the next morning, Karan and Yuvan, filled with anticipation, prepared for their journey to Karan's home. As they arrived, Karan's mother stood at the doorstep with their pet dog Tobi, her eyes bright with excitement, ready to welcome them with open arms. She had spent hours preparing for their visit, ensuring that everything was just perfect, especially for Yuvan, whom she was meeting after twelve years.

"Welcome, Yuvan! It's so lovely to finally meet you," Karan's mother exclaimed, her smile infectious as she ushered them inside.

Yuvan was touched by her warmth and the effort she had put into making them feel at home. The house was filled with the aroma of freshly cooked food, and the table was set beautifully, a testament to her hospitality.

"Thank you for having me, aunty. Everything looks wonderful," Yuvan said, genuinely grateful for her kindness.

"From that brave little boy, you've grown into such a charming young man, Yuvan," Karan's mother exclaimed, her eyes shining with pride and excitement. Her words echoed in Yuvan's heart, filling him with a deep sense of gratitude for the journey that had led him to this moment. As they enjoyed the meal, Karan's mother and Yuvan engaged in a heartfelt conversation.

"You know, Yuvan, Karan never mentioned he was searching for you all these years," Karan's mother said, her tone filled with curiosity. Yuvan was surprised.

"He didn't? I had no idea," he replied, intrigued by the revelation.

"Yes, it's quite amusing actually. Your dad and Karan's dad are still in contact. If Karan had just mentioned it, it would have been so easy for him to find you," Karan's mother explained, shaking her head with a smile.

Yuvan chuckled, a mixture of surprise and amusement in his voice. "That's quite the coincidence. I guess sometimes, the simplest solutions are right in front of us," he mused.

Karan's mother nodded, her eyes twinkling with amusement. "Indeed. But then again, if everything had been easy, you wouldn't be enjoying this thrill of a reunion, would you?" she said, her words carrying a profound wisdom

. Yuvan smiled, touched by her perspective. "You're right. I suppose everything happens for a reason, even if we don't always understand it at the time," he replied, grateful for the twists and turns that had led him back to Karan.

As they continued their meal, Yuvan felt a deep sense of gratitude for the unexpected journey that had brought him here, to this moment of connection and friendship. He knew that this reunion was more than just a coincidence; it was a reminder that sometimes, the most beautiful moments in life come from the most unexpected places. In that moment, he realized that he had not only found a friend in Karan but a second family as well, and for that, he was truly grateful.

CHAPTER XIV

Echoes of Trust

Late in the evening, as the sun dipped below the horizon, Yuvan and Karan made their way to Dr. Ravi Mehta's office. Dr. Mehta, Karan's trusted psychiatrist and Tej's father, greeted them warmly.

"Hello, Doctor. How are you?" Karan inquired, a hint of anticipation in his voice.

"I'm good, I'm good. And this must be Yuvan," Dr. Mehta replied, his eyes twinkling with recognition.

"Yes, that's him. Yuvan, meet Dr. Ravi, my psychiatrist from childhood and also Tej's dad," Karan introduced, a sense of pride evident in his voice.

"It's a pleasure to meet you, Doctor," Yuvan said, extending his hand.

"Likewise, Yuvan. You're actually a hero in Karan's mind. Do you know that?" Dr. Mehta remarked, a smile playing on his lips.

Yuvan chuckled, "I guess I had an idea."

As they settled into the room, Dr. Mehta turned to Yuvan with a gentle smile. "Karan, if you don't mind, could you give us fifteen minutes alone? I'd like to have a chat with Yuvan about that unforgettable day," he requested.

"Of course, Doctor. I'll wait outside," Karan said, understanding the need for privacy.

"Thank you, Karan," Dr. Mehta said as Karan left the room. Alone with Yuvan, Dr. Mehta's demeanor softened.

"Yuvan, are you comfortable?" he asked, his tone warm and inviting.

"Yes, I am," Yuvan replied, feeling a sense of ease in the doctor's presence.

"Yuvan, as I mentioned, Karan has complete faith in you. Do you know why?" Dr. Mehta asked, a sense of intrigue in his voice.

Yuvan looked at the doctor, his curiosity piqued. "Perhaps you don't recall, but when you rescued him from the kidnappers, you said something that left a lasting impact on him," Dr. Mehta explained. "You promised to always stand by his side, to protect him, and to kick anyone's ass for him. Those words have stayed with Karan all these years. If anyone can help him overcome his fears, it's you."

Yuvan was moved by the doctor's words. "I will do my best. I want to help him," he replied earnestly.

"Believe me, Yuvan, your presence has already made a significant difference in Karan's life. He came for a session after meeting you, and I haven't seen him that happy in years," Dr. Mehta revealed, a sense of gratitude in his voice.

His eyes welled up with tears, mirroring the turmoil in his heart. He was overwhelmed with a deep sense of regret, wishing he could turn back time and change the moments he couldn't recognize Karan. He felt a renewed sense of purpose, a determination to support Karan in every way possible.

With a reassuring pat on the shoulder, Dr. Mehta offered his support. "I trust you, Yuvan. Together, we can make a difference in Karan's life." As Yuvan stepped outside, he felt a renewed sense of responsibility. He was ready to embark on this journey of healing and friendship, knowing that he had the support of not just Karan and Dr. Mehta, but also a newfound sense of purpose within himself.

CHAPTER XV

A Night of Healing and Renewal

Yuvan and Karan spent a splendid evening with Karan's parents, sharing stories and laughter. After dinner, Karan's mom expressed a desire for Yuvan to bring his parents to visit sometime soon.

Late into the night, as everyone retired to their rooms, Yuvan found himself unable to sleep. He wandered out to the balcony, hoping the night air would calm his restless mind. On his way, he noticed Mrs. Gupta stepping out of Karan's room.

"Is everything alright?" Yuvan asked, concerned.

"Yes, he's fine. Karan has trouble sleeping alone; he needs a companion. That's Tobi, our dog, with him. He's afraid of the dark and has insomnia, all stemming from that terrible kidnapping. I deeply regret what happened," Mrs. Gupta confided.

Yuvan listened intently, unable to find the right words to comfort her.

"I'm sorry, I shouldn't have burdened you with this. You should get some rest," Mrs. Gupta said, breaking the silence.

Yuvan bid her goodnight and then knocked on Karan's door. Karan, surprised, opened it.

"I can't sleep. Can I share your bed tonight?" Yuvan asked softly.

As Karan stood puzzled, Yuvan gently took his wrist and switched off the light.

"Yuvan, what are you doing? Please turn on the light; I'm scared," Karan's voice quivered, his body breaking into a cold sweat despite the cool air from the AC. In response,

Yuvan wrapped his arms around Karan in a warm, comforting hug, his touch a balm to Karan's fears.

"You're going to be alright. I'll be right here with you tonight. Trust me, don't worry," Yuvan whispered reassuringly. "Come, let's go to bed." With great care and tenderness,

Yuvan guided Karan to bed, ensuring he was comfortable. He gently cradled Karan in his arms, softly patting his head in a soothing rhythm. Karan's breathing gradually slowed, the tension easing from his body as he fell into to a peaceful sleep, safe and secure in Yuvan's embrace. The next morning, Yuvan woke early, feeling refreshed. Downstairs, Karan's mother offered him coffee, noticing his contemplative expression.

"What's on your mind, Yuvan?" she asked. Yuvan's recount of the previous night was filled with a mix of emotions.

"I'm not sure if what I did was right or wrong, but after you left, I went to Karan's room, persuaded him to turn off the light, and slept beside him. Remarkably, he slept peacefully through the night, without a single disturbance. He's still asleep now," Yuvan shared, his eyes reflecting both amusement and sorrow. "It's the first time I've had to comfort someone with such deep-seated trauma. The thought of him searching for me for twelve years is heart-wrenching. I can't imagine how much he must have suffered alone."

Mrs. Gupta listened intently, her expression filled with regret. "You're right. I failed to protect him that day, and he still can't fully trust me. I regret it deeply," she admitted sadly. Just then, Karan entered the room, his face adorned with a gentle smile. His mother inquired about his sleep, to which he responded,

"It was wonderful. I think I slept better than ever." Yuvan and Mrs. Gupta exchanged a meaningful glance, filled with satisfaction and joy. They shared a beautiful breakfast together, and as Yuvan and Karan bid farewell to the Gupta family, there was a palpable sense of healing and renewed trust in the air.

CHAPTER XVI

Fearless Adventure! A Journey of Trust

Yuvan returned home, his heart heavy with the weight of the previous night's events. He felt compelled to share everything with Dr. Mehta, the psychologist who had been guiding him through Karan's trauma. As he sat across from Dr. Mehta, he recounted the story, every detail tinged with emotion. To his surprise, Dr. Mehta's eyes filled with admiration and appreciation for Yuvan's deep empathy and understanding.

"Yuvan," Dr. Mehta began, "your compassion for Karan is truly remarkable. I believe we can delve deeper into his trauma through further experiments. Your dedication to helping him is admirable." Yuvan felt a sense of validation and purpose.

With Dr. Mehta's guidance, he knew he could make a difference in Karan's life. The next morning, Yuvan called Karan, his voice gentle yet filled with excitement.

"Hello, how are you, Karan?" Yuvan asked, eager to share his plan.

"I'm well. Why did you call me?" Karan's voice held a hint of curiosity.

"I'm planning a special trip for just the two of us next weekend. Would you be interested?" Yuvan's voice was warm with anticipation. "Just you and me?

Are you sure?" Karan sounded pleasantly surprised.

"Trust me, it's a journey meant only for us. I haven't mentioned it to anyone else," Yuvan assured him.

"You've already done so much for me. Why are you doing this?" Karan's voice was filled with gratitude.

"To be honest, I regret not being there for you sooner. I want to help you heal from your past. Let's face this together. Can you trust me?" Yuvan's words were sincere, filled with a desire to make amends. "Hello, can you hear me?" Yuvan's voice was gentle, seeking reassurance.

"Yes, I'm listening, Yuvan... I truly appreciate what you're doing for me. But, I never want to be a burden or a botheration to you," Karan replied softly.

"You could never be a burden, Karan. I cherish every moment with you. Will you come with me?" Yuvan's voice was filled with hope.

After a moment of contemplation, Karan said, "Yuvan, I trust you. But, I'm scared of adventures. I'm afraid I'll spoil your mood."

"Don't do it for me, do it for yourself. Do you want to come out of this fear? See this as an opportunity to overcome it. Trust yourself and come with me. What do you think?" Yuvan encouraged warmly.

"Hmmm... I'm in. Let me give it a try," Karan finally agreed, a hint of excitement in his voice

. That weekend, Yuvan and Karan embarked on their much-anticipated trip on Yuvan's bike, a symbol of their shared journey ahead. As they rode through winding roads, Karan's initial fear gradually melted away, replaced by a sense of adventure and curiosity. Both wearing helmets, Karan held onto Yuvan's waist, their closeness a testament to the trust and bond between them.

The scenic beauty that surrounded them was nothing short of enchanting. Lush greenery enveloped them, and the sound of cascading waterfalls filled the air with a soothing melody. Playful monkeys added a touch of whimsy to the landscape, making Karan feel like he had stepped into a fairy tale.

Despite the initial apprehension, Karan found himself embracing the journey with an open heart. The beauty of the surroundings captivated his senses, and he couldn't help but marvel at the wonders of nature. With each passing mile, he felt a sense of liberation, as if the wind itself was carrying away his fears and worries.

As they rode on, the misty clouds above added a touch of mystery to the adventure, casting a magical spell over the landscape. Karan's heart was filled with gratitude for this moment of escape, this moment of pure joy and freedom. Their journey was not just about reaching a destination; it was about the experiences they shared along the way.

It was a journey of self-discovery, of overcoming fears, and of forging a bond that would last a lifetime. And as they reached their destination, Karan knew that this trip would forever hold a special place in his heart. By the time they reached their destination in the evening, Karan was a different person.

The resort welcomed them with its serene ambiance and breathtaking views. Surrounded by nature's beauty, Karan felt a sense of peace and tranquility wash over him. The weekend was filled with moments of laughter, exploration, and bonding. Yuvan and Karan enjoyed each other's company, relishing in the simple pleasures of life.

As they returned home, Karan felt grateful for the experience and the newfound courage he discovered within himself. Their trip was not just a physical journey but also a journey of self-discovery and healing. It was a testament to the power of trust, friendship, and love to overcome even the deepest of fears.

CHAPTER XVII

Heartfelt Confessions

Days passed, and Yuvan and Karan continued with their daily routines, but something was clearly troubling Karan. Unable to contain his thoughts any longer, he made his way to Yuvan's condo, only to find it empty. Knowing Yuvan was at his part-time job, Karan decided to wait for him outside, sitting silently in front of his door. When Yuvan returned home from work, he was startled to find Karan waiting for him outside his condo.

"Karan, you scared me! Ohh," Yuvan exclaimed, clearly taken aback by the unexpected encounter.

"I'm sorry, I didn't mean to scare you. I just wanted to talk to you. I didn't want to disturb you while you were working, so I waited here," Karan explained softly, his eyes filled with sincerity and a hint of apprehension.

"Come inside," Yuvan invited warmly, stepping aside to let Karan enter. Karan entered the apartment, his heart pounding with a mix of nervousness and determination.

"Sit here. Relax and tell me the matter. Your face is telling me you are perplexed by something. You can tell me what is going on in your mind. Then only I can help you. So, take this juice, drink it, make yourself comfortable, and talk to me," Yuvan said, offering Karan a can of juice with a gentle smile.

Karan struggled to relax, his mind racing with thoughts and emotions.

Sensing his friend's unease, Yuvan asked, "Do you want me to take you for a ride and talk in some other place?"

"No, no need for that. Just give me some time," Karan replied, his voice betraying a hint of vulnerability.

"Well then, I am going to take a shower. Just relax yourself," Yuvan said reassuringly before heading to the bathroom, leaving Karan alone with his thoughts. As Yuvan stepped out of the bathroom, he found Karan standing there, eyes closed, his words hanging heavy in the air.

"Yuvan... I think I am falling for you. I just want to stop my feelings. Can we not talk to each other?" Karan's voice was filled with anguish, his heart laid bare.

Yuvan's heart clenched at Karan's words. He had never imagined this moment would come, yet here it was, unraveling before him. Stepping closer, he gently cupped Karan's face, urging him to open his eyes. As Karan's eyes fluttered open, Yuvan was met with a mixture of vulnerability and fear.

"Can we stop talking?" Karan asked, his voice barely above a whisper, the pain evident in his eyes.

"Do you really want that?" Yuvan asked softly, his heart aching at the thought of losing the connection they shared. Karan hesitated, his emotions swirling inside him.

"I... I don't know. I just... I can't handle these feelings," he confessed, his voice breaking. Yuvan took a deep breath, steeling himself to reveal his own truth.

"Karan, there's something you need to know. I... I am gay. You're the only one who knows, apart from my male friends," he admitted, his voice filled with raw honesty. Karan's eyes widened in surprise, and he took a moment to process this revelation.

"But what about Esther?" he asked, his voice tinged with concern.

Yuvan smiled softly, reaching out to hold Karan's hand. "Esther is my best friend, nothing more. My feelings for you are real," he said, his voice filled with sincerity.

Karan felt a rush of emotions overwhelm him. "I always felt like she likes you," he confessed, his voice barely above a whisper. Yuvan gently brushed a stray lock of hair from Karan's face.

"Even if she does, it doesn't change how I feel about you. You're the one I want to be with," he said, his eyes shining with love.

Before Karan could process it all, Yuvan leaned in and gently pressed his lips against Karan's, a tender gesture filled with unspoken emotions. Karan's eyes widened in surprise, but he didn't pull away. Instead, he closed his eyes, allowing himself to feel the warmth of Yuvan's lips against his own. As they pulled away, Yuvan looked into Karan's eyes, his own filled with love and longing.

"I don't want to stop talking to you, Karan. I want to be with you, to explore this connection between us," Yuvan confessed, his voice filled with sincerity.

Karan felt a surge of hope and relief wash over him. "I want that too, Yuvan," he said softly, a small smile tugging at the corners of his lips. "I want to be with you."

In that moment, as they stood there, wrapped in each other's arms, Yuvan and Karan knew that their lives had changed forever. They had found love in the most unexpected of places, and they were ready to embrace it, together. As they stood there, their hearts entwined in a moment of pure honesty and vulnerability, Karan knew that Yuvan's love was genuine. And in that moment, he felt a sense of peace and acceptance wash over him, knowing that they could face whatevcr challenges lay ahead, together.

CHAPTER XVIII

Poisoned Bonds

As Yuvan and Karan grew closer, Esther started feeling jealous of their bond. Although Karan sensed her jealousy, he knew that for Yuvan, their friendship was purely platonic. Despite being Yuvan's best friend, he had never shared his secret of being gay with Esther, and she had never suspected it. Karan remained unaffected by her jealousy, trusting in the strength of his relationship with Yuvan.

One day, Yuvan invited Karan to join him at a pub where all their friends would be. Yuvan hoped this outing would help Karan overcome his fear of crowds. Initially hesitant, Karan agreed at Yuvan's insistence and the encouragement of their friends.

To everyone's surprise, Esther was also at the pub. Yuvan, always attentive to Karan's needs, stayed by his side to ensure he felt comfortable and at ease. Esther, having learned of their plan beforehand, had already arrived at the pub. She offered drinks to Yuvan and Karan, keeping one for herself. For fun, Yuvan swapped the drinks around a few times before they started drinking.

While Karan and Yuvan began to drink, Esther excused herself to use the restroom. From there, she messaged Yuvan, claiming that her parents had unexpectedly arrived at her condo and she needed to rush home. Relieved, Yuvan told Karan that Esther had left. However, Yuvan soon noticed a difference in the taste of his drink and started feeling dizzy.

Karan sensed something was wrong and insisted on taking him to the hospital.He also made sure to ask one of Yuvan's friends to bring the remaining drink from Yuvan's glass to the hospital for testing. At the hospital, tests confirmed that Yuvan had been poisoned, and he was admitted to the ICU for twentyfour-hour observation.

Karan's quick thinking had saved Yuvan's life. Yuvan's and Karan's parents rushed to the hospital upon hearing the news. Mr. Reddy's friend, who was a detective, began investigating the case to uncover the culprit behind the poisoning. In the midst of this crisis, the bond between Yuvan and Karan grew stronger as they faced this ordeal together, reaffirming their love and commitment to each other.

As the police inspector began to interrogate, Karan was the first to be questioned. The atmosphere in the room grew tense, with an air of anticipation hanging heavy. Karan sat upright, his expression composed yet resolute, ready to face the scrutiny of the inspector's questions. He recounted the events of that fateful night.

"What made you think of taking him to the hospital and the balance glass of the drink Yuvan was drinking?" the officer asked, his tone serious.

"I don't trust Esther," Karan replied without hesitation.

"Why is that?" the officer inquired, leaning forward slightly.

"I know she's been feeling jealous of my relationship with Yuvan. It's no secret that she has a crush on him," Karan explained. "I have a video that shows her true colors. In one of our first encounters, I gave Yuvan a lollipop. Esther, being clever as she is, took it from him and threw it in the trash without anyone noticing."

The officer listened intently, taking notes as Karan spoke. "I also believe that Yuvan wasn't the target that night; it was me," Karan concluded, a steely resolve in his eyes.

"Thank you for your cooperation, Karan. We'll get back to you if we need more information," the inspector said, acknowledging Karan's statement.

Esther was next to be questioned by the inspector.Esther sat nervously as the inspector questioned her about the events leading up to Yuvan's hospitalization.

"Why did you go to the pub uninvited?" the officer asked, his gaze piercing.

"I knew Yuvan and his friends were going, so I thought it would be fun to join them," Esther replied, her voice trembling slightly. "But I couldn't enjoy myself. I received a call and had to leave immediately."

"Did you drink your drinks that day?" the officer inquired, his tone neutral.

"No, I didn't," Esther replied, her eyes avoiding the inspector's gaze.

"Why not?" the officer pressed, sensing there was more to her story.

"I planned to use the restroom first and then drink it afterward. But I received a call and had to rush home," Esther explained, her voice tinged with regret.

"When did you learn about the incident?" the officer asked, noting her responses.

"I saw Aditya's message the next day, and I was shocked," Esther replied, her hands fidgeting nervously in her lap.

"Did you go to see him?" the officer questioned further, trying to gauge her reactions.

"No, I didn't," Esther admitted, her voice barely above a whisper. "When I called Aditya, he said Yuvan was in the ICU. Even if I went, I couldn't see him."

"Lastly, do you have feelings for Yuvan?" the officer asked, observing Esther's reaction closely.

"Honestly, yes," Esther replied, her eyes welling up with tears.

"Thank you for your cooperation, Esther. We'll get back to you if we need more information," the inspector said, concluding the questioning.

As Yuvan remained in the ICU, the inspector was unable to question him directly. This added a layer of complexity to the investigation, as Yuvan's firsthand account could have provided crucial insights into the events leading up to his poisoning. Instead, the inspector had to rely on the statements of those present at the pub that night and other evidence to piece together the sequence of events.

CHAPTER XIX

Shadows of Emotion

After two days in the ICU, Yuvan was finally moved to a room where Karan took on the role of his primary caregiver. Tej, Karan's close friend, also lent a helping hand to Karan in looking after Yuvan's needs.

That evening, as Karan was coming out of the washroom, Esther entered the room. Although she had come to visit Yuvan, her expression quickly turned to one of anger when she saw Karan there. Without a word of greeting, Esther's voice rose in a sharp and accusatory tone, causing Karan to panic at her sudden outburst.

"How dare you!" she exclaimed, her words dripping with contempt. "Do you think you can just waltz in here and play the caring friend after what you've done? You're nothing but bad luck to him! Why do you insist on being here? Can't you see that you're only making things worse?" Each word was like a dagger, piercing Karan's heart and leaving him feeling utterly helpless. He tried to block out her harsh words by closing his ears, but they echoed in his mind, filling him with fear and panic. He sank to the floor, overwhelmed by the weight of her accusations, unsure of how to respond.

"Esther, you need to stop. If you're unaware, then let me make it clear: he is my world, the love of my life. You have no right to utter a word against him," Yuvan's voice resonated with a potent mix of anguish and fury. "You caused him distress. I can never forgive you for this, Esther. You're no longer a friend to me. Leave this room now." Yuvan's words cut through the air like a sharp blade, his unwavering love and protection for Karan palpable in every syllable.

Tej, sensing the escalating tension, rushed to call the nurse. He also called his father, Dr. Mehta, explaining the situation and asking for his advice.

As Esther left the room, tears streaming down her face, she was filled with regret for her outburst. She knew she had let her emotions get the best of her and had hurt her friends deeply.

Dr. Mehta, Karan' s psycatrist, arrived at the room and gave Karan proper treatment for his panic attack. He advised both Yuvan and Karan to rest and assured Tej that he would take care of them.

As Yuvan sat in his hospital room, surrounded by his loved ones, the atmosphere suddenly shifted as the inspector arrived to record his statement. Sensing the tension in the air, the inspector inquired about the situation, prompting Tej to explain the events that had transpired.

"Are you in a condition to give your statement, Yuvan?" the inspector asked, his voice gentle yet probing.

"Yes, I am," Yuvan replied, his voice steady despite the turmoil within him.

The inspector then requested everyone to leave the room, wanting to ensure privacy for the interrogation. Once they were alone, he began, "Can you explain what happened that day?"

Yuvan recounted the events as best as he could recall, his words painting a vivid picture of the evening's events. "I remember feeling dizzy and disoriented after drinking the cola that Esther had given us," he explained.

"Have you noticed anyone suspicious?" the inspector inquired, leaning forward attentively.

"No, I didn't notice anything out of the ordinary," Yuvan replied, furrowing his brow in thought.

"Do you believe someone deliberately poisoned you?" the inspector pressed, his eyes focused intently on Yuvan.

"I can't say for certain, but it seems likely,"

Yuvan admitted, his mind racing with the possibilities.

The inspector then shifted his line of questioning. "How would you describe your relationship with Karan and Esther?"

"I trust Karan completely. He was by my side throughout the evening. In fact, I was the one who encouraged him to join us. Karan has a fear of crowds due to a past incident, so going to a pub was a big step for him. I held his hand, offering him comfort and support. I have absolute faith in him," Yuvan replied confidently.

"And Esther?" the inspector continued.

"Esther was my best friend," Yuvan began, his voice tinged with a hint of sadness. "Karan and I both knew that she had feelings for me. However, as I was not romantically interested in her, I didn't pay much attention to it," he explained.

The inspector nodded, taking notes as Yuvan spoke.

"Did you notice anything unusual about her behavior that day?" the inspector inquired.

"I didn't see anything strange. Esther was the one who gave us drinks," Yuvan said, his voice softening as a realization struck him. He paused, a hint of surprise on his face, before meeting the inspector's gaze with newfound clarity.

The inspector smiled and asked, "Is there anything else you'd like to add?"

Yuvan, his mind still puzzling over the events, shook his head. "No, nothing else at the moment," he said.

The inspector nodded, taking note of Yuvan's observation. "Thank you for your cooperation, Yuvan. We will investigate further and get back to you if needed," he concluded, offering Yuvan a reassuring smile before taking his leave.

As the inspector departed, Yuvan was left with a lingering sense of unease. He knew that finding the truth behind his poisoning would not be easy, but he was determined to uncover the answers, for his own sake and for the safety of those he cared about.

It was a dark day for all, a day filled with raw emotions and painful realizations. The bonds of friendship and love were tested, leaving everyone involved with a sense of sadness and regret.

CHAPTER XX

Bound by Love

As Yuvan was discharged from the hospital, he was greeted by Karan's parents, who had been anxiously waiting for this moment. Yuvan's parents were also there, relieved to see their son well again.

"Thank you for taking care of Yuvan," Yuvan's mother said, embracing Karan's parents warmly.

"It was the least we could do. Karan means a lot to us," Karan's father replied, patting Yuvan on the back.

Yuvan hesitated for a moment before speaking. "Mr. and Mrs. Reddy, I was wondering if it would be possible for Karan to stay with me for a while. I want to make sure he's okay and help him recover."

Karan's parents exchanged a glance, then smiled at Yuvan. "Of course, Yuvan. We trust you to take care of him. Just let us know if you need anything."

Yuvan nodded gratefully. "Thank you. I promise I'll take good care of him."

As they left the hospital, Yuvan felt a sense of relief knowing that he could be there for Karan during his recovery. He knew that with his love and support, Karan would soon be back to his old self.

As Karan's primary caregiver, Yuvan took on the responsibility of tending to his every need. He made sure that Karan took his medication on time, helped him with daily tasks, and encouraged him to rest and recover.

Despite the turmoil and uncertainty surrounding them, Yuvan and Karan's bond grew stronger. They found solace in each other's presence, drawing strength from their love and commitment to one another.

As days turned into weeks, Karan began to slowly heal, both physically and emotionally. Yuvan's unwavering support and love played a crucial role in his recovery, helping him regain his confidence and sense of security.

They faced the future together, knowing that they could overcome any challenge as long as they had each other.

The incident at the hospital had tested their relationship, but it had also reaffirmed their love and commitment to each other. Yuvan and Karan emerged stronger than ever, ready to face whatever life threw their way, knowing that together, they could conquer anything.

It was a bright morning, and Karan was finally returning to college after a month of rest.

"Tej, can I count on you to look after him?" Yuvan texted Tej, concerned about Karan's first day back.

"Absolutely, you can count on me," Tej replied promptly, offering his support.

"I'll be there to pick him up after his class," Yuvan reassured, wanting to ensure Karan's smooth return.

"Okay," Tej replied, grateful for Yuvan's support.

Meanwhile, as Yuvan was preparing for his class, his phone rang. It was his dad.

"Hi dad, how are you?" Yuvan asked, answering the call.

"Good. Tell me, where are you and Karan?" Mr. Reddy inquired.

"We are at the college. Why do you ask?" Yuvan responded, curious about his father's inquiry.

"Don't panic, but I have some news for you. It's confirmed that Esther is the mastermind behind the poisoning," Mr. Reddy confirmed, his tone serious.

"What?" Yuvan exclaimed in shock, unable to believe what he was hearing.

"Karan was her target. She asked the bartender to mix poison in his drink, disguising it as medicine. The inspector is on the way to arrest her. Remember, this is confidential," Mr. Reddy explained, his voice filled with concern.

"Dad, I...I don't know what to say," Yuvan stammered, his mind reeling from the revelation.

"Dad, just think about it. If it had been Karan, he wouldn't have noticed the taste difference. It could have been disastrous. He always mentioned not trusting her, and now we understand why. How could she do something like this?" Yuvan's voice trembled with panic and disbelief, struggling to comprehend the gravity of Esther's actions.

"Sometimes, love can be more than we can handle, and that's when things get dangerous," Mr. Reddy replied, his tone somber. "It's a harsh truth, but it's important to accept it and move on."

"I understand, but it's still unbelievable. I can't imagine her like this," Yuvan said, his voice filled with sadness.

"Just accept the reality and move on. That's what I want to say," Mr. Reddy advised, his voice reassuring.

"Dad, I'm hanging up. I need to see Karan right now," Yuvan said, ending the call abruptly. He ran to Karan, embracing him tightly and sobbing uncontrollably.

"Yuvan, what's wrong? Why are you crying?" Karan asked, returning the hug.

Tej intervened discreetly, hinting to Yuvan that their emotions were attracting attention.

"I can't bear the thought of life without you, Karan. Please, always be with me," Yuvan said, his voice filled with anguish.

"I love you, Yuvan. I'll always be here," Karan reassured him.

An hour later, news spread that Esther had been arrested at home for poisoning Yuvan. As the truth emerged, everyone understood the depth of Yuvan's emotions and his need to hold onto Karan.

52

CHAPTER XXI

Embracing the Night

Yuvan lay awake, troubled by Esther's betrayal and unable to shake off the fear for Karan's safety. Sensing his restlessness, Karan spoke softly, "Can't sleep?"

"No," Yuvan replied, his voice filled with worry. "I can't bear the thought of anything happening to you."

Karan smiled gently, "Don't worry about me. I'm safe. You're the one I'm worried about."

" I know you've never been fond of Esther. Now I understand why," Yuvan mused, his tone gentle.

Karan turned to him, his eyes reflecting a mixture of sadness and understanding. "Even if you didn't see it, I could sense something wasn't right with her. She never truly accepted us," Karan shared, his voice filled with a mix of vulnerability and strength.

Yuvan reached for Karan's hand, intertwining their fingers. "You deserve unwavering acceptance and love, Karan. I'm sorry you had to endure her negativity," Yuvan whispered, his eyes full of empathy and love.

A soft smile graced Karan's lips, his gaze locked with Yuvan's. "I have that love and acceptance with you, Yuvan. That's all that matters. You..are the light of my life, the one I choose to live with till the end of my life," he said, leaning in to share a tender kiss.

Yuvan tried to speak, but Karan silenced him with a tender kiss on the lips, reassuring him of his love and safety.

Karan's touch was a lifeline, grounding him in the present moment.

As the night progressed, Karan gently traced his fingers along Yuvan's cheek, his touch sending a shiver down Yuvan's spine. "You mean everything to me, Yuvan. I can't bear the thought of anything happening to you," Karan whispered, his voice filled with sincerity.

Yuvan looked into Karan's eyes, seeing nothing but love and devotion. "And you mean the world to me, Karan. I never want to lose you," Yuvan replied, his voice full of emotion.

Their lips met in a tender kiss, a silent promise of their love and commitment to each other. The warmth of their embrace was a comforting balm to Yuvan's troubled heart, soothing away his fears and doubts.

As they lay together in the darkness, their bodies entwined, Yuvan felt a sense of peace wash over him. In Karan's arms, he found solace and security, knowing that no matter what challenges they faced, they would always have each other.

Their love was a beacon of light in the darkness, guiding them through the night and into a new day filled with hope and possibility.

CHAPTER XXII

Forevermore

Years passed swiftly, and Yuvan now serves as a Wing Commander in the Air Force, while Karan dutifully follows in his father's footsteps, assisting him. Despite the distance, Yuvan and Karan maintain a strong and loving relationship. Karan's recent visit to Yuvan after a business tour with his dad was a testament to their enduring bond, as they eagerly reunited after their time apart, cherishing every moment together.

As Karan's flight landed, Yuvan stood eagerly at the airport, his heart racing with anticipation. He spotted Karan walking towards him, and their eyes met, sparking a wave of emotions. They embraced tightly, both feeling the warmth of each other's presence after what seemed like an eternity.

"I missed you so much," Yuvan whispered, holding Karan close.

"I missed you too, more than words can express," Karan replied, his voice filled with love and longing.

As they drove back home, their hands intertwined, neither wanting to let go. The next day, as they woke up together, Yuvan couldn't contain his excitement. He had planned something special for their sixth year of togetherness.

Yuvan had planned something special for the evening. He had arranged a romantic dinner at their favorite restaurant, overlooking the city skyline. The atmosphere was perfect, with soft music playing in the background and the twinkling lights of the city below.

As they enjoyed their meal, Yuvan couldn't wait any longer. He took Karan's hand in his and looked deeply into his eyes. "Karan, these six years with you have been the best of my life. I can't imagine my life without you by my side. Will you marry me?"

Karan's eyes widened in surprise, and then a smile spread across his face. "Yes, Yuvan, a thousand times yes!" he exclaimed, tears of joy welling up in his eyes.

Yuvan slipped an attractive engagement ring onto Karan's finger, and they embraced, knowing that their love was forever.

After dinner, they returned to their hotel room, where Yuvan had arranged a surprise. The room was decorated with candles and rose petals, creating a romantic ambiance. They spent the rest of the night lost in each other, reaffirming their love and commitment to each other.

As the night progressed, Yuvan and Karan's passion for each other grew stronger. They continued to express their love through gentle caresses and tender kisses, each touch igniting a fire within them. Their kisses became more intense, fueling the desire that had been building between them.

Unable to resist any longer, Yuvan and Karan gave in to their desires. They undressed each other slowly, savoring every moment of anticipation. As they came together, their bodies melted into one, moving in perfect harmony. It was a moment of pure bliss, where time seemed to stand still.

Afterwards, as they lay in each other's arms, their hearts beat as one. They knew that their love was strong and true, and that no matter what challenges lay ahead, they would face them together.

As they lay in each other's arms, basking in the afterglow of their love, Yuvan whispered, "I love you more than words can say, Karan. You are my everything."

"And you are mine," Karan replied, kissing Yuvan softly, their hearts overflowing with love and happiness.

They drifted off to sleep, content in the knowledge that they had found true love in each other.

CHAPTER XXIII

A Love as Bright as the Decor

The sun rose on a day filled with excitement and love, as Yuvan and Karan prepared to exchange vows. The venue was a sight to behold, adorned with vibrant flowers of every hue. Garlands of marigolds, roses, and jasmine adorned the entrance, leading the guests into a space transformed into a fragrant garden of love.

Yuvan, resplendent in a sherwani of vibrant colors of purple and golden, stood at the altar, his heart brimming with anticipation. As the music began to play, signaling Karan's arrival, Yuvan's eyes sparkled with joy. Karan, looking every bit the prince charming in a classic Ivory and gold Sherwani and dupatta, walked towards Yuvan, their eyes locked in a gaze that spoke volumes.

As they stood facing each other, the priest began the ceremony, invoking the blessings of the Gods for their union. Yuvan and Karan exchanged vows, their voices a melody of love and commitment.

"I promise to always stand by your side, to support you, and to love you unconditionally," Yuvan vowed, his voice filled with unwavering determination.

"And I promise to stand by you, to cherish you, and to love you with all my heart, for all eternity," Karan replied, his voice filled with a depth of emotion that touched everyone's hearts.

Their friends, Aditya, Neel, Raj, and Tej, looked on with smiles, their hearts filled with happiness for the couple.

"Yuvan, Karan, your love is an inspiration to us all. May it continue to grow stronger with each passing day," Aditya remarked, raising his glass in a heartfelt toast.

Neel nodded in agreement. "Indeed, your love is a testament to the power of love itself. May your bond be as enduring as the mountains and as deep as the oceans."

Raj added, "Yuvan, Karan, may your life together be a grand adventure, filled with love, laughter, and endless joy."

Tej clapped Yuvan on the back. "Cheers to the grooms! May your love story be as timeless and beautiful as the stars above."

Their parents, Mr. and Mrs. Reddy, Mr. and Mrs. Gupta, and Dr. Mehta, approached them, their eyes shining with tears of joy.

"Yuvan, Karan, you have our blessings. May your life together be as radiant and joyful as this day," Mr. Reddy proclaimed, embracing them both.

"Karan, we are so happy to have you as part of our family. May your love for each other continue to blossom and grow," Mrs. Gupta declared, her voice filled with emotion.

"Yuvan, you have brought so much happiness into Karan's life. You are truly a remarkable person," Dr. Mehta commended, his voice filled with admiration.

The evening continued with music, dance, and laughter, as Yuvan and Karan celebrated their love surrounded by the people who mattered most to them. It was a night of pure magic, a night that would forever be etched in their hearts as the beginning of their happily ever after.

CHAPTER XXIV

A Night of New Beginnings

As the wedding festivities came to a close, Yuvan and Karan retreated to their room, their hearts full of love and anticipation for the night ahead. The room was decorated with candles, casting a warm, inviting glow. Yuvan took Karan's hand in his, leading him to the center of the room.

"Tonight is the beginning of our new journey together, my love," Yuvan said, his voice filled with tenderness. "I want to cherish every moment with you."

Karan gazed into Yuvan's eyes, his own eyes shimmering with emotion. "Meeting you and being with you always is the greatest gift life has ever bestowed upon me," he whispered, his voice filled with a longing that had been building for years. "I have waited so long for this moment, to be with you, to love you completely."

Yuvan's heart swelled with love as he took Karan's hands in his. "And I have waited a lifetime to hold you like this, to feel your heart beat against mine," he murmured, his voice soft with emotion.

Yuvan wrapped his arms around Karan, pulling him close. "I love you more than words can express. "You are my everything, Karan. Tonight, I want to show you just how deeply I love you." he said, his voice filled with promise.

As they embraced, their love filled the room, enveloping them in a warm, comforting cocoon. They shared their hopes, dreams, and fears, laying bare their souls to each other in a way they never had before.

"I promise to always be here for you, to support you, and to love you with every fiber of my being," Yuvan vowed, his words a solemn pledge.

"And I promise to stand by you, to cherish you, and to love you for all eternity," Karan replied, his voice filled with sincerity and love.

Their love blossomed that night, transcending the physical and becoming something truly magical. It was a night of new beginnings, of deep, abiding love, and of promises made from the depths of their hearts.

As they lay in each other's arms, the room filled with a sense of peace and contentment. They knew that their love was strong enough to weather any storm, to overcome any obstacle. They were bound together not just by love, but by a deep, unbreakable bond that would last a lifetime and beyond.

CHAPTER XXV

A Love Beyond Measure

As the sun set on their wedding day, Karan made a heartfelt decision—to prioritize his time with Yuvan above all else. He gracefully managed his business from afar, ensuring that only urgent matters drew him away from their shared happiness.

Their love blossomed in the tranquil moments they spent together, exploring the vibrant cityscape of their lives. They visited Yuvan's workplace at the Indian Air Force, where the Government provided them with a home and all the comforts they could wish for. Each day felt like a new adventure, a new chapter in their fairy-tale love story.

As their life together blossomed, Karan started a new branch of his business near their current place of residence. He flew back to his hometown when his father needed him, managing their business from his new office.

Time seemed to dance around them, and before they knew it, a year and a half had passed, a testament to their unwavering bond. One day, news of Yuvan's mother's illness brought them back to reality. They rushed to her side, where Karan's heart was touched by the sight of a mother and her newborn baby, igniting a deep longing in him.

Driven by their shared dreams, they embarked on a journey to fulfill Karan's wish for a family. They found a surrogate mother, and the following year, their joy knew no bounds as they welcomed fraternal twins, Ishan and Jay, into their lives. The resemblance of the twins to each of them was a beautiful reminder of their love.

Returning from a blissful family vacation, they were greeted with warmth and love from their families. Ishan and Jay brought a new kind of happiness, filling their home with laughter and love.

As Yuvan continued to soar in his career, now an Air Commodore in the Indian Air Force, his passion for flying was matched only by his love for Karan and their two adorable kids. Their life together was a testament to the power of love, proving that with unwavering support and a deep bond, they could conquer any challenge that came their way.

And so, their story continued, a beautiful melody of love, happiness, and endless possibilities, reminding us all that true love knows no bounds and that family is the greatest gift of all.

Miss Hazel sighed softly, her eyes reflecting the warmth of the tale she was about to share. "This is their story. "The family is currently enjoying a well-deserved vacation, visiting their relatives in a picturesque town. Karan is here with us for the time being, tending to business deals."

The new receptionist, deeply touched by the story, responded with genuine awe, "Oh, my! I'm truly speechless, feeling a mix of awe and admiration for their journey. I wish everyone could experience such a supportive family. The way their parents supported their children's wishes is truly admirable. With two adorable kids now, their story is a true testament to love and family."

Miss Hazel smiled, her heart swelling with joy. "Their journey is truly inspiring. Their unwavering love and support for each other, along with their families, have created a beautiful life."

As the sun began to set, casting a golden glow over the room, Miss Hazel and the receptionist shared a moment of quiet appreciation. It was a reminder that with love, anything is possible.

And so, the story of Yuvan and Karan continued, a beacon of hope and inspiration for all who heard it. Theirs was a tale of love, family, and the enduring power of togetherness.

"Their journey reminds us that love and family are not just important, but essential aspects of life, capable of bringing us through the darkest of times."

www.ingramcontent.com/pod-product-compliance
Lightning Source LLC
Chambersburg PA
CBHW031505150726
47990CB00007B/2875